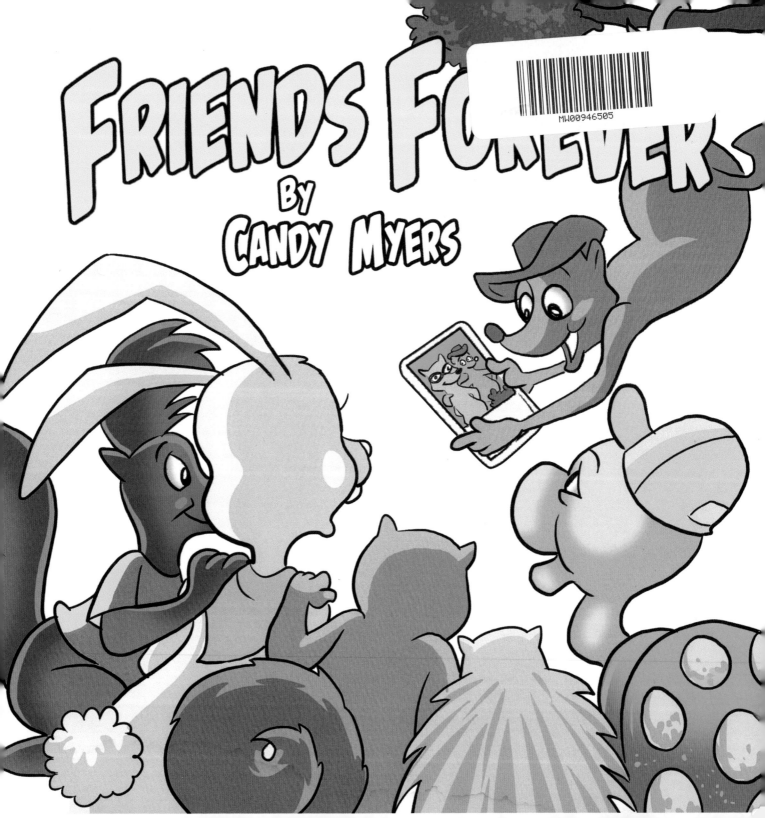

ISBN-13: 978-1499221619

FRIENDS FOREVER

By
CANDY MYERS

illustrated by MikeMotz.com

Tap! Tap! Tap!

"Go away! Leave me alone!"
Tully Turtle yelled from inside his shell.

"Tully, you can't stay inside forever,"
his friend Skippy Skunk replied.

"He's right!" other forest friends echoed.

Along with Skippy, Stanley Squirrel,
Pamela Porcupine, and Felicity Fox had gathered
around Tully to wait for their other friends.

This was the time of day the forest critters
liked to play games together.

Tully slowly inched his head to the front of his home.
Two tear-filled eyes peered out of the
opening at his friends.

"You do-do-don't un-derst-a-a—and," Tully cried brokenly.

"My —y b-best fr-ie-nd h-as m-m-oved.
I -I m-iss Fran-k-ie Fr-og."

"Oh, Tully!" Stanley Squirrel said.

"Remember when Chucky Chipmunk had to go
live with his grandparents in another forest?"

"Yeah! And you were the one," Felicity Fox interrupted,
"who told Stanley he could stay in touch
and continue being friends."

By this time, Tully had completely come out of his shell.
He listened as his pals began to repeat some of the same
things he and the others had said to comfort Stanley.

"We talked about all the different ways we could communicate with Chucky and remain close to him," Pamela Porcupine said.

As Pamela was speaking, the rest of the gang — Rosita Rabbit, Ricky Robin, Ollie Owl, and Perry Opossum — had arrived.

The forest friends began recalling the different ways to support long distance friendships.

"Talking on our cell phones," Ricky Robin tweeted.

"Also texting," Perry Opossum uttered, while hanging by his tail on a tree branch.

"Emailing on our computers," Skippy Skunk said.

"Don't forget the coolest way of all!"
Rosita Rabbit stated excitedly while hopping up and down.
"Skyping on our iPads! My absolute favorite!"

"Hey! Recall how we imitated what our parents
and grandparents have said at least a hundred times,"
Felicity Fox said, as she began to speak in a deep,
adult voice. "You kids don't know how good you have it.
Back in my day we didn't have all this technology.
Some of us didn't even have phones."

"Oh, and don't forget this," Perry Opossum interjected in his slow drawl. "What if you had lived when sending telegrams was the main way to contact someone?"

"And what about the Pony Express!" Ollie Owl hooted.
"It could be months and months or even a year
before hearing from someone."

By this time, Tully and his forest friends were talking and laughing at the same time while mimicking their parents and grandparents.

After a few minutes when everyone had settled down, Tully spoke. "Thank you for being my friends and cheering me up from feeling sorry for myself. We're all going to miss Frankie, not just me!"

"Also, let's not forget that when Chucky Chipmunk moved away, we talked about the most important way to stay close," Skippy Skunk said.

"Memories!" they all spoke at once.

"He will always live in our hearts," Skippy continued on, "just like Frankie Frog will!"

"Every time we play Hide-and-Seek, Tag, or other games,"
Pamela Porcupine added, "we'll think of both Frankie
and Chucky and all the fun we had."

"We also need to remind ourselves that both Chucky and Frankie have it much harder than we do!" Ricky Robin chirped.

"That's right! We've still got each other. Chucky had to make new friends just like Frankie will have to do now!" Perry Opossum added.

"That's why every night I say a special prayer for Chucky Chipmunk," Stanley Squirrel said on a serious note.

"I say a prayer every night for my family and all my friends," Felicity Fox added.

The other forest friends agreed that they did, too.

"I want to remind all of you how wonderful everyone was to me when my family and I relocated here last year," Perry Opossum said. "At first, I felt miserable until all of you kept asking me to play and be a part of your group."

"What about the friends you left?" Rosita Rabbit asked. "I just realized that I've never asked you about any of them. Have any of the rest of you talked to Perry about his friends from where he moved?"

All of the forest friends looked around sheepishly at each other while shaking their heads "no."

"We're sorry!" they all spoke at once.

"That's okay," Perry said. "But maybe in the future if someone new moves here, that's something we can do."

"That's a great idea!" Pamela Porcupine declared.

The rest shook their heads in agreement.

"Well, since I don't believe it's ever too late to correct a problem," Ollie Owl hooted wisely, "tell us about the friends you left and how you have been communicating with them."

"Yeah!" the others echoed.

Over the next few minutes, Perry couldn't talk fast enough about his other friends. He even showed them their pictures on his new iPhone that he had just received for his birthday. Everyone was enjoying Perry's stories.

While the group had been talking, they hadn't noticed
that someone had quietly moved within listening distance.

"Excuse me," a soft voice called.

All of the friends turned to look to see who had spoken.

"Hello, I'm Lizzie, and I hope you're serious
about what you were saying."

"Welcome, Lizzie Lizard!" the group, grinning from ear to ear, said in unison.

"You've definitely moved to the right forest,"
Tully Turtle stated. "And you're IT!"

They all started laughing as they began to play Tag.
And could Lizzie ever run!

"A friend loves at all times,..."
Proverbs 17:17 (NIV)

Made in the USA
Charleston, SC
20 May 2014